封
交通
封
und Hanako-Kun
D0125206

Contents

FISH
SPIRIT
封
SEAL
SPOOK 16
THE LITTLE MERMAID (PART 1)

AH-HA!

STRIDE

SURPRISED?

I HAVE A REALLY GOOD ASSISTANT TOO.
SHE HELPED ME MAKE IT HERE.

SO, AMANE—
す
SFF

PATCH: SEAL

ARE YOU...

RUB

...HAPPY TO SEE ME?

AH...

TMP

HANAKO-KUN!!

WHAM

MELT
ドロ
WOW ...

YOU'RE PRETTY GOOD.

WSHH
EEK...

...HUH?
ニコ
GRIN

SEE YOU LATER.

THAT... BOY...
ヘナヘナ
TREMBLE
TREMBLE
...HANAKO-KUN.
フラ...
SWAY

IS HE...
...THE PERSON YOU KILLED...?
ぎゅ
TUG

WHAAM
OW...!!

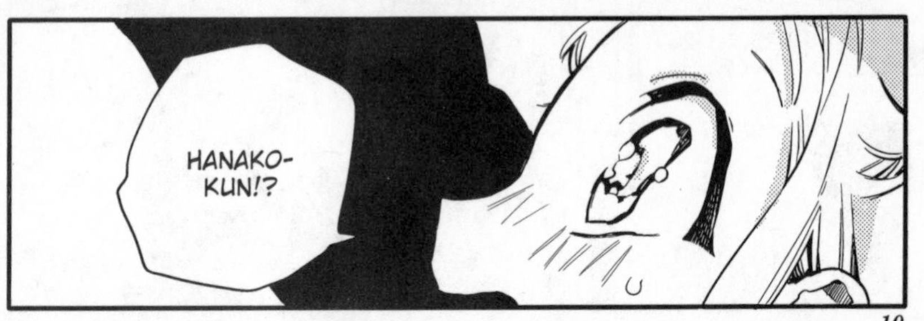
HANAKO-
KUN!?

WH—

WHAT'S WRONG...?

...!

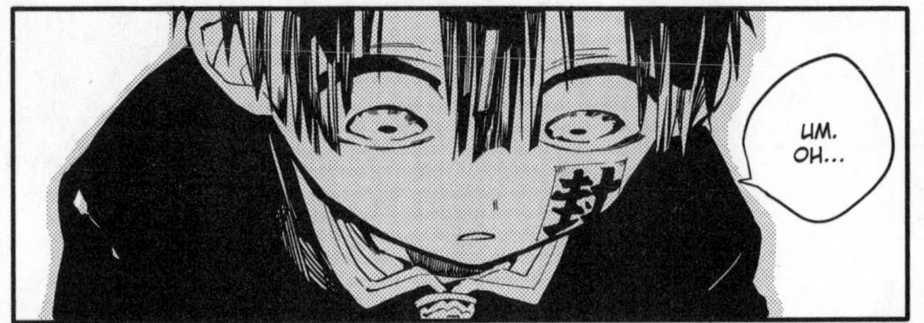

SORRY...

......I'M SORRY.

WOBBLE

I...

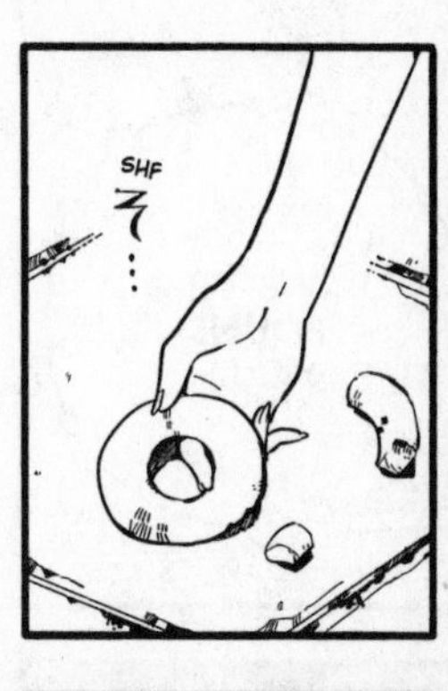
SHF
そ…

CLENCH
ぎゅっ

SPLISH
ちゃぷん

WE'VE FOUND YOU...
...MY LADY.
とぷん
SPLISH
キーン
DIING
コーン
DOOONG
カーン
DAAANG
コーン
DOOONG
BOX: YAHOO! TEA
...I GUESS...
...PEOPLE FROM DIFFERENT SPECIES REALLY CAN'T UNDER-STAND EACH OTHER...

NENE-CHAN...
GULP
ゴクリ...
WHAT HAVE YOU FALLEN IN LOVE WITH THIS TIME?
DONUTS ...
DONUTS !?
MAYBE IT WOULD'VE BEEN BETTER IF I WERE A SUPERNATURAL TOO...

OH-HO? YOU WISH TO BECOME A SUPER-NATURAL?
WELL, WELL. HOW VERY CONVENIENT.
ALLOW US TO GRANT YOUR WISH...!

FWIP
ぱっ
WHO'S THERE?
WHO'S TALKING TO ME...!?
N-NENE-CHAN...
OH! DOWN HERE!
WE ARE BENEATH YOU!

IT IS OUR DEEPEST PLEASURE TO MAKE YOUR ACQUAINTANCE ...
GLUUUB プカ〜
...MY LADY.
F—
CLATTER ガタン!!
FISH !!!
MURMUR ざわ...
MURMUR ざわ...
WHAT'S WRONG...?
"FISH"?
WHAT WAS THAT?
ARE YOU OKAY...?
SFF す

DASH

だっ

NENE-CHAAAN!!?

I'LL HAVE YOU KNOW...

...I AM THE ASSISTANT TO THE LEADER OF THE SEVEN MYSTERIES!
AND I'M FRIENDS WITH A REALLY POWERFUL EXORCIST!

SO—I HAVE NO IDEA WHAT YOU ARE...
...BUT IF YOU LAY A FIN ON ME...

ビッ
FWIP

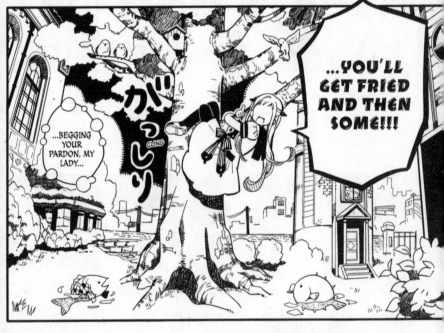

...YOU'LL GET FRIED AND THEN SOME!!!

がっしり

CLING

...BEGGING YOUR PARDON, MY LADY...

...BUT YOUR CLAIMS HARDLY SEEM CONVINCING...
IT'S TRUE!!
ユサ
SHAKE
ユサ
SHAKE

• • •

WELL THEN, MY LADY—
YOU MAY STAY RIGHT WHERE YOU ARE, BUT PLEASE HEAR WHAT WE HAVE TO SAY.

WE HAVE COME TO RELEASE YOUR HONORABLE PERSON...
...FROM THE CLUTCHES OF THAT LOATHSOME SCHOOL MYSTERY.
MM-HMM!
MM-HMM!

RELEASE ME FROM HANAKO-KUN...?
WHY WOULD YOU FISH DO SOMETHING LIKE THAT...?

WITHIN YOUR BODY DWELLS A PIECE OF THE FLESH OF OUR MASTER, THE GREAT MERMAID.
YOU MEAN... THOSE SCALES?
SEE VOL. 1, SPOOK 1.
YES.
ZMM
ZMM
NOM

OUR LAW STATES THAT THOSE WHO HAVE EATEN THE FLESH AND BLOOD OF OUR MASTER...
...WILL EVENTUALLY BECOME OUR NEXT MASTER.
ERGO...

PRINCESS
...YOU, MY LADY, ARE OUR PRINCESS.
PRINCESS!?
YOU ARE EXTRAORDINARILY BEAUTIFUL, MY LADY.
MM-HMM!
MM-HMM!
IT WOULD SEEM THAT THE HUMAN CHILDREN HAVE NO EYE FOR BEAUTY...
...BUT IF YOU WERE TO COME TO OUR WORLD...
...YOU WOULD BE ROYALTY!
COMBINE THAT WITH YOUR RARE, UNEQUALED BEAUTY...
...AND YOU WOULD REEL IN A NEW MAN WITH EVERY CAST OF YOUR LINE!
HAREM
ハーレム
GULP
ゴクリ…
E-EVERY CAST...!?

COULD I GET A LITTLE MORE DETAI—
SNAP
EEK!

THUD
ドスン…
ビク
WINCE
ビク
WINCE

OUCH…
AND, MY LADY…
…THIS WOULD ALSO BE FOR YOUR OWN BENEFIT.

WE'VE BEEN WATCHING YOU THESE PAST FEW DAYS…
…AND THAT SCHOOL MYSTERY'S TREATMENT OF YOU IS FAR TOO BARBARIC.
TREMBLE
TREMBLE
ワナワナ
KEH HEH HEH!
IMAGE
MM-HMM!
MM-HMM!

HE DIDN'T EVEN ACCEPT THE GIFT YOU HAD SO THOUGHTFULLY PREPARED FOR HIM…
AND THEN, TO BEHAVE WITH SUCH VIOLENCE…

TH-THAT WAS…

HE NEVER SHARES A WORD ABOUT HIMSELF...
...AND HE TAKES ADVANTAGE OF YOU AT EVERY POSSIBLE TURN!

THAT VILE OFFENDER THINKS NOTHING OF YOU, MY LADY!

STING ズキ

THAT'S NOT...

DESPITE APPEARANCES, OUR MASTER IS VERY KIND.
AND UNLIKE THAT KNAVE, WE HAVE GREAT LOVE AND RESPECT FOR YOU.

HERE—PLEASE ACCEPT THIS.

THIS IS THE GREAT MERMAID'S LIFEBLOOD.
キラ
SPARKLE
キラ
SPARKLE
PLEASE DRINK IT WITHOUT DELAY.

IN DOING SO...
...YOUR HORRID BOND WITH THAT SCHOOL MYSTERY WILL BE OVER-WRITTEN...
封
封
...AND YOU WILL BE FORMALLY BOUND TO THE GREAT MERMAID.

IF I DRINK THIS, I CAN BREAK MY BOND WITH HANAKO-KUN...?
PRECISELY.

AND THEN, YOUR HONORABLE PERSON...
...WILL CEASE TO TRANSFORM IN REACTION TO WATER.
!

O PITIFUL PRINCESS...

...COME WITH US! IT WILL BRING YOU HAPPINESS.

WE WILL RETURN TO ESCORT YOU HOME WITH US ON THE MORROW.

SPLOOSH
FARE THEE WELL!

SIGN: SCIENCE PREP ROOM 2

第二理科準備室

......

WHAT SHOULD I DO...?

A SERVANT TO THE MERMAID?

WELL...
...WHY NOT?
WHAAT!? WHY WOULD YOU SAY THAT!?
BLUNT
進路調査

I CAME HERE TO GET YOU TO STOP ME!!
THE PRINCESS TREATMENT, NO EXPERIENCE REQUIRED, NO ACADEMIC BACKGROUND OR QUALIFICATIONS REQUIRED...
SOUNDS GOOD TO ME.
CREEEAK

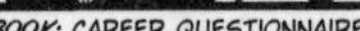
BOOK: CAREER QUESTIONNAIRE

THAT'S THE PROBLEM— IT DOES SOUND GOOD!!
PAIN IN THE...
WAAAH!

HAVE YOU TALKED TO HONORABLE No. 7 AND MINAMOTO?
NO, I HAVEN'T.
IT WOULD BE TOO AWKWARD TO TALK TO MINAMOTO-KUN AFTER I RUINED THE DONUTS WE MADE TOGETHER.

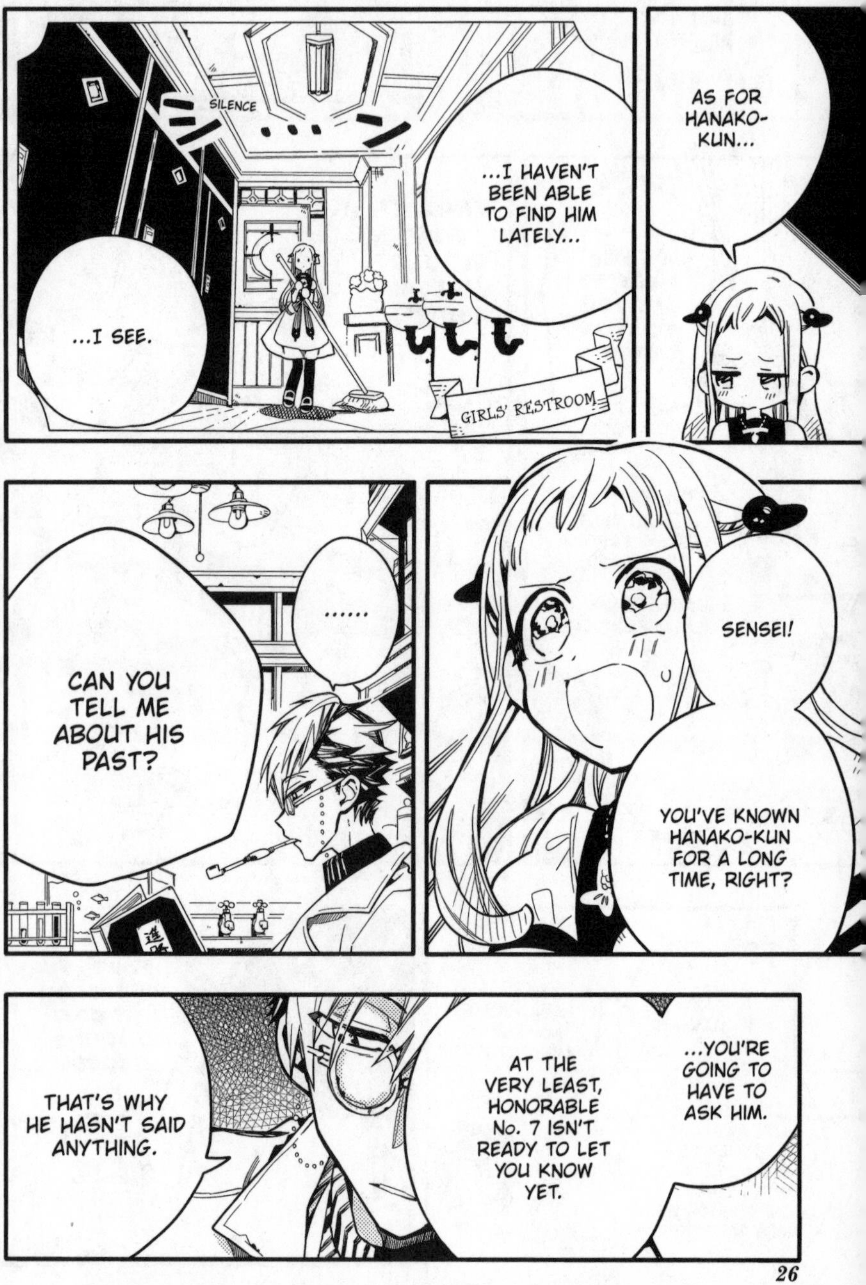

AS FOR HANAKO-KUN...

...I HAVEN'T BEEN ABLE TO FIND HIM LATELY...

SILENCE

...I SEE.

GIRLS' RESTROOM

SENSEI!

YOU'VE KNOWN HANAKO-KUN FOR A LONG TIME, RIGHT?

......

CAN YOU TELL ME ABOUT HIS PAST?

...YOU'RE GOING TO HAVE TO ASK HIM.
AT THE VERY LEAST, HONORABLE No. 7 ISN'T READY TO LET YOU KNOW YET.
THAT'S WHY HE HASN'T SAID ANYTHING.

...BUT WHY WON'T HE TELL ME?
IS IT 'COS...HE DOESN'T TRUST ME...?

IT'S PROBABLY 'COS, IF YOU KNEW, YOU'D STOP BEING SO SWEET TO HIM!
YOU'RE ALWAYS BABYING HIM...!
GYA HA HA!
MAKING HIM DONUTS...

EITHER THAT...

...OR HE'S AFRAID OF YOU FINDING OUT.

JUST...
...MAKE SURE YOU DON'T REGRET IT.

PATTER
PATTER
PATTER
...

...SO? WHAT'RE YOU GONNA DO...

...HONORABLE No. 7?

FLIT

......

じゃ〜ん
TA-DAA
NOW, MY LADY!
PLEASE HONOR US WITH A RESPONSE TO OUR OFFER FROM THE OTHER DAY!!

I'M VERY SORRY!

ぱっ
BLUNT

BUT I JUST CAN'T CUT MY TIES WITH HANAKO-KUN!!

WH-WHAT!?

I KNOW YOU'D GIVE ME SPECIAL TREATMENT, BUT IT DOESN'T MATTER.
I CAN'T JUMP SHIP WHEN I'M STILL IN THE MIDDLE OF THIS.

IT'S TRUE HANAKO-KUN MIGHT JUST BE USING ME...
MAYBE HE DOESN'T THINK ANYTHING OF ME...

BUT... I WANT TO BELIEVE THAT'S NOT THE CASE.

M-MY LADY, PLEASE THINK THIS THROUGH MORE RATIONALLY!
I KNOW! YOU, THERE! BRING THE IMAGES!
YES, RIGHT AWAY!

I-IMAGES? LIKE PHOTOS OF THOSE HOT MERMEN YOU TOLD ME ABOUT YESTERDAY?
H-HMM...I'M NOT REALLY INTERESTED, BUT...
チラ
GLANCE

BAM

魚拓ゥ!!

FISH PRINTS!!

YES! WE MADE INK RUBBINGS OF THEM!

—PRINCE KNIFEJAW

SENDING ALL MY LOVE...

—HIS LORDSHIP ANGELFISH

SHAKE MY FIN IN A SEA FULL OF BEAUTIFUL CORAL...

—AMBASSADOR ANGLER

COME TO ME!

MM-HMM!

MM-HMM!

FISH!

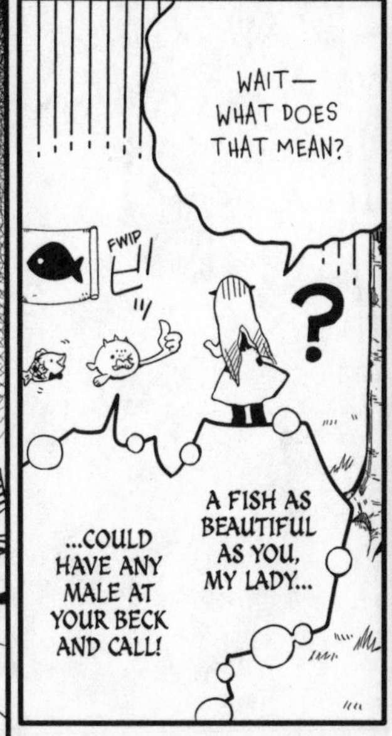
WAIT— WHAT DOES THAT MEAN?
FWIP
A FISH AS BEAUTIFUL AS YOU, MY LADY...
...COULD HAVE ANY MALE AT YOUR BECK AND CALL!

WHAT? BEAUTIFUL FISH...?
SWAY

SPLOOSH
GLUB
!!
FWSH
AHHH, SHE TRULY IS BEAUTIFUL!

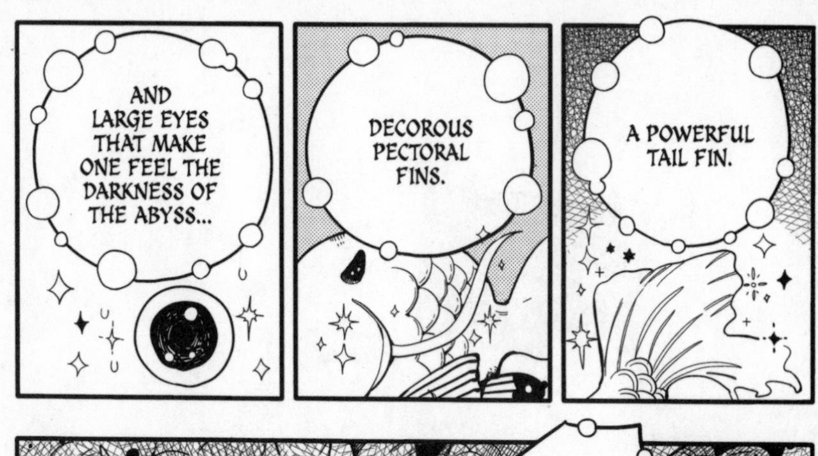
A POWERFUL TAIL FIN.
DECOROUS PECTORAL FINS.
AND LARGE EYES THAT MAKE ONE FEEL THE DARKNESS OF THE ABYSS...

WAIT A MINUTE!
WHEN YOU SAID BEAUTIFUL— DON'T TELL ME YOU MEANT FISH-ME!?
FORSAKE THOSE BEASTLY LEGS AND COME WITH US!
TO OUR WORLD OF FISH!!

THEY'RE ACTUALLY A TEACHER AND HIS STUDENTS.
HOW TO BECOME A FINE PUFFER FISH!
MM-HMM.
MM-HMM.
SPECTER No. 003
MERMAID SERVANTS
Servants of the Millennia-old supernatural known as the Mermaid. They've come to take Nene, who was cursed after swallowing the scales of their master, to their world as the new heir to the throne.

封
封
SPOOK 17
THE LITTLE MERMAID (PART 2)

SPLOOSH

NOW COME, OUR PRINCESS!

FORSAKE ALL...

...AND BECOME PART OF OUR WORLD!

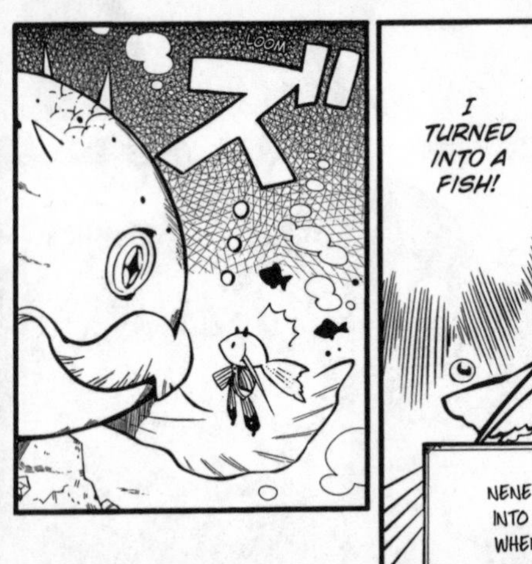

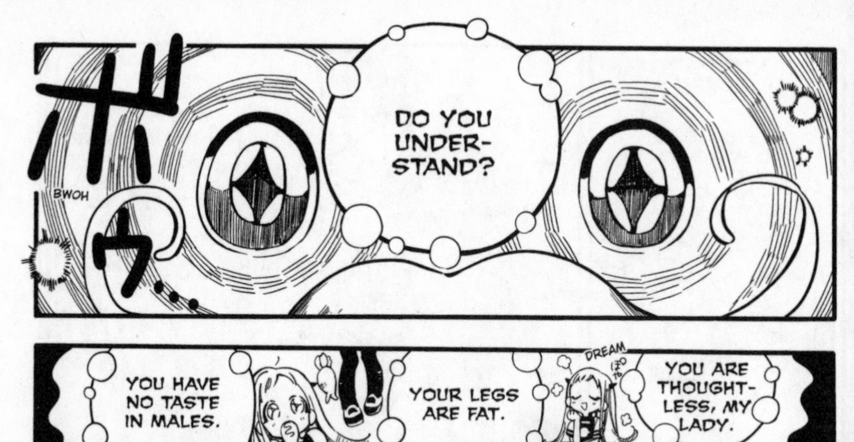

DO YOU UNDER-STAND?
BWOH
YOU ARE THOUGHT-LESS, MY LADY.
DREAM
YOUR LEGS ARE FAT.
YOU HAVE NO TASTE IN MALES.

YOU ARE TRULY AN UTTER FAILURE IN MATTERS OF LOVE!!
KACRACK
I—
I-I-I-I-I-I—
WOOZY
I AM NOT......
WOOZY

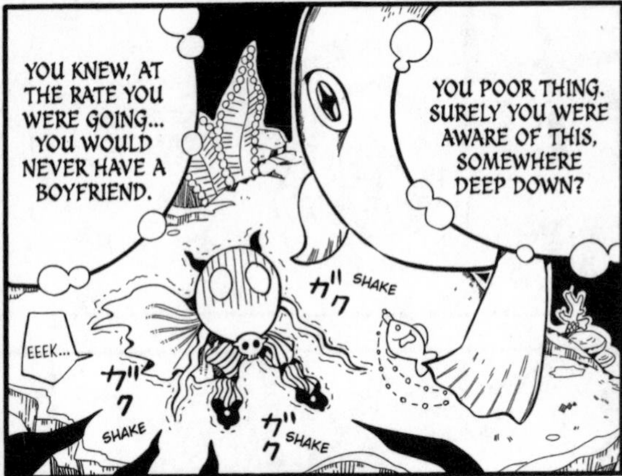

YOU POOR THING. SURELY YOU WERE AWARE OF THIS, SOMEWHERE DEEP DOWN?
YOU KNEW, AT THE RATE YOU WERE GOING... YOU WOULD NEVER HAVE A BOYFRIEND.
SHAKE
EEEK...
SHAKE
SHAKE

THERE, THERE. IT'S NOTHING TO BE TROUBLED OVER NOW.

YOU WERE MERELY BORN INTO THE WRONG WORLD.
THE DRIED-UP WORLD OF THE NEAR SHORE, AND THOSE TWO GHASTLY LEGS.
IF YOU WERE TO THROW THEM ALL AWAY...

...AND DO US THE HONOR OF COMING TO OUR WORLD...

FLOAT

IN A WORD, YOU WOULD BE POPULAR!!
PRINCE KNIFEJAW
NENE-SAMA!
NE...NE... SAMA...
NENE-SAMA!
COME TO ME!
MY LADY IS MY LIFE
HIS LORDSHIP ANGELFISH
AMBASSADOR ANGLER
...YOU WOULD REIGN AS QUEEN!
TOP OF THE POPULARITY PYRAMID!
I'D BE... POPULAR?
YES!
NOW PLEASE TAKE THE GREAT MERMAID'S LIFEBLOOD...
キュポ POP
DON'T.

?
SCOOP
SPLAAASH
WAAAAAAAAH!!!?
TOSS
EEK!

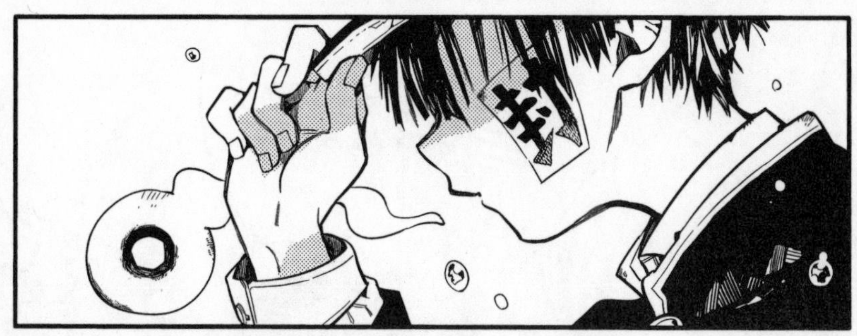

YOUR WORLD MAY BE KIND TO HER...
...AND SHE MAY NOT HAVE AN EASY LIFE HERE...
EEEEEK!
FALL
...BUT IT DOESN'T MATTER.

BECAUSE
YASHIRO
LIKES ME.

H...
HANAKO-KUN...

ニコ
GRIN

S-SCHOOL MYSTERY!
あーっ
SHOUT
MM-HMM!
MM-HMM!
LET MY LADY GO!!

COME ON...

WE CAN'T HAVE THIS KIND OF BEHAVIOR...
DIDN'T YOUR MASTER TEACH YOU NOT TO TAKE THINGS THAT DON'T BELONG TO YOU?
WHAT!?

ビッ
FWIP
IF YOU GET TOO FULL OF YOUR-SELVES...

...I'LL TURN YOU INTO SASHIMI. GOT IT?

FLUTTER

SASHIMI

SOY SAUCE

WASABI

E—
EEEEK! MAAASTER ...!!
JUMP
JUMP
JUMP
CLAAANG
ACK! YOU COWARDS!!

GRR! HOW VEXING...
CONFOUND YOU, SCHOOL MYSTERY! WE WILL NEVER GIVE UP!
TREMBLE
TREMBLE
TREMBLE
MM-HMM!
MM-HMM!

MY LADY!
UNTIL WE MEET AGAIN!
ZOOOOM

BYE-BYEEE!

SILENCE
....
CAW!
CAW!

H... HANAKO-KUN...
UM...
I... WASN'T GOING TO GO WITH THEM...
YOU DID THINK A HAREM WOULD BE KINDA NICE THOUGH, DIDN'T YA?
STARE
GULP
URK!
I-I'M SORRY.

...
...I'M JUST JOKING.
I'M THE ONE WHO SHOULD BE SORRY.
WHAT?

YOU MADE ME THOSE DONUTS...
FIDGET
もぞ
SORRY I RUINED THEM...
もぞ
FIDGET

WILL YOU FORGIVE ME?

......

YES!

AND—
THANK
YOU.
?

WIPE
ごし

I FORGOT TO SAY IT BEFORE.
I'VE...
...NEVER HAD A GIRL TELL ME SHE LIKES ME BEFORE.

IT MADE ME HAPPY.
BADUM
ドキ
BADUM
ドキ
BADUM
ドキ
Y—
YEAH...

YOU KNOW, I...

I HAD A YOUNGER BROTHER.
SQUEEZE
ギュウ…

BUT I KILLED HIM.
SO, YASHIRO ...
DO YOU... REALLY WANNA GET TO KNOW ME?
IF YOU DO...
...THEN, SOME-DAY...
...I'LL TELL YOU EVERY-THING.
封

BE MY ASSISTANT UNTIL THEN, OKAY?

......

OKAY!

立入禁止

NO TRESPASSING
放送室
BROADCAST ROOM
立入禁止
ヒソ PSST
ヒソ PSST

SWIVEL
ぎょろ
PSST
ヒソ
...WAS THAT REALLY A GOOD IDEA?
PSST
PSST
ヒソ!

PSST
PSST
ヒソヒソ
SWIVEL
ギョロ
LETTING THE RUNT GO OFF AND DO WHATEVER HE WANTS.
PSST
PSST
ヒソヒソ
IT'S FINE.
IF I'D TRIED TO STOP HIM, HE WOULDN'T HAVE LISTENED ANYWAY.
ヒソヒソ
PSST
PSST

BOOK: LAWS GOVERNING URBAN LEGENDS: BOUNDARIES WITHIN CITIES

BUT IF THEY FIND OUT WE'RE THE ONES CHANGING THE RUMORS ...

...THE THREE OF THEM...
EXORCIST
ASSISTANT
SCHOOL MYSTERY CHARGED WITH MAINTAINING CORRECT RELATIONSHIPS BETWEEN HUMANS AND SUPERNATURALS
...MIGHT COME AFTER US, RIGHT?

WHEN THAT HAPPENS...

...YOU'LL PROTECT ME, WON'T YOU...
...NATSU-HIKO?
!

SFF
す

BUT OF COURSE!
PLAYAAA...
MMM...
MY LA—

WHAP
—DY!!?

DON'T TOUCH ME.
YES, MA'AM... I'M SORRY...
PSST
PSST
WHIRL
OH!

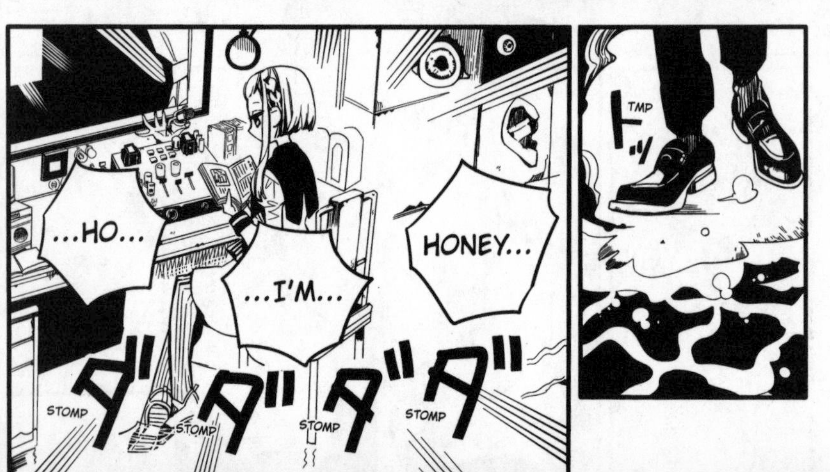
TMP
HONEY...
...I'M...
...HO...
STOMP
STOMP
STOMP
STOMP

CLOMP
がばーっ
GRAAAAAH!!
...OOOME!!
ダン
WHAM
THAT'S AN UNUSUAL OUTFIT.
YEAH, WEEELL...

I MEAN, I WAS SEEING AMANE FOR THE FIRST TIME IN AGES!
WHIIIRL
ヒュ
SO YOU SPECIFICALLY WORE THAT TO MATCH YOUR BIG BROTHER?

YUP. ♥

HE LOOKED HAPPY TO SEE ME!
REALLY.
I'M HAPPY FOR YOU.
BUT I STILL CAN'T MOVE AROUND THAT WELL YET.
THEY CHASED ME OFF.
フヨ〜
FLOOOAT

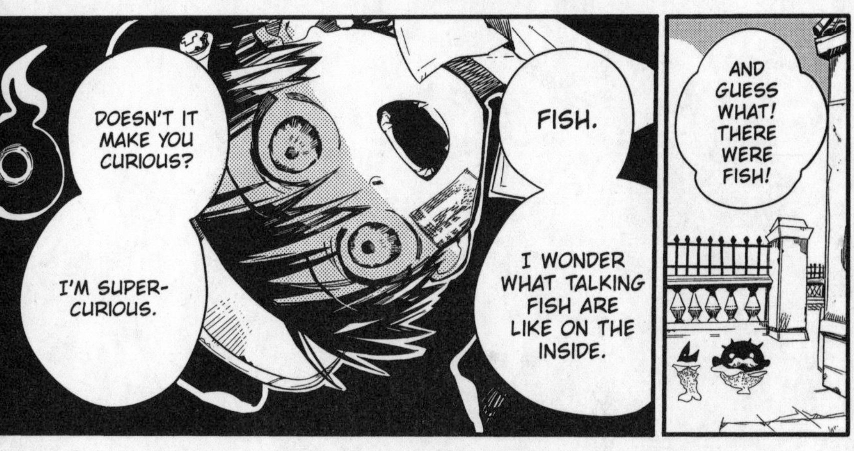
AND GUESS WHAT! THERE WERE FISH!
FISH.
I WONDER WHAT TALKING FISH ARE LIKE ON THE INSIDE.
DOESN'T IT MAKE YOU CURIOUS?
I'M SUPER-CURIOUS.

SOOO— ARE YOU?
COME ON, TELL ME! YOU'RE CURIOUS, AREN'T YOU?
TELL ME, TELL ME, TELL ME, TELL ME!
I DON'T CARE.
LET GO OF HER!

COME ON, LET'S JUST GET THOSE RUMORS GOING...
AH HA HA!
ALL RIGHT, ALL RIGHT.
OKAY, SAKURA...

...WHAT RUMOR SHOULD WE SPREAD TODAY?

LET ME THINK...

SNEAK
SPLISH
WE'VE FOUND HIM!

THE SUPER-NATURAL WHO WAS ON THE ROOF THE OTHER DAY!!

THE SCHOOL MYSTERY SEEMED WARY OF THIS ONE...

IF WE CAN GET HIM TO JOIN OUR SIDE...

..THEN MAYBE WE CAN CROSS SWORDS WITH THE KNAVE!

ALL FOR MY LADY!
MM-HMM!
MM-HMM!

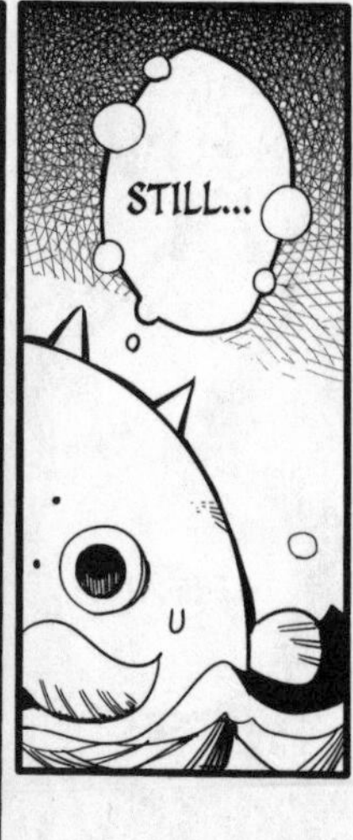

STILL...

...WHY IS HIS FACE IDENTICAL TO THAT ACCURSED SCHOOL MYSTERY'S?
AND WHAT IS HE DOING HERE?
HE SAID SOMETHING ABOUT SPREADING RUMORS...?

OUR MASTER TOLD US THE RUMORS OF NEAR-SHORE SUPERNATURALS HAVE BEEN IN DISARRAY OF LATE.
COULD IT BE THEY ARE—?
?

HEY.
AIEEE!
ビクーーッ
WIIINCE

WHAT ARE YOU?
ぴち
FLOP
ぴち
FLOP
ぴち
FLOP
U-U-U-UNHAND ME!
I AM OF THE HIGH AND NOBLE WATER PEOPLE!

AND IT'S TALKING ...
MY LADY, I THINK WE'VE BEEN SPOTTED.
BY THIS FISHY THING...

FISH!

CLATTER
カタ
IT'S NOT REALLY A PROBLEM.
LET IT GO.
AS YOU WISH!
HFF
HFF
SWIPE
AH?

C-C-C-CEASE AND DESIST! DO NOT TREAT ME SO VIOLENTLY!
POKE
POKE
AHA! IT'S TALKING!
PLOP
WHADDAYA THINK TALKING FISH ARE LIKE...

...ON THE
INSIDE?

...DON'T
KILL IT.

クルッ
TWIRL

OH, DON'T
WORRY!
ナデ
PET
ナデ
PET

I'M JUST GONNA TAKE A LITTLE PEEK!
封
EEP!
GEEZ...
YUCK
I TOLD YOU NOT TO DO THAT...

IT'S BEEN GROWING SLOWLY SINCE THE INCIDENT.
A TREE WITH A FACE...
GRATIN.
BROCCOLI GRATIN...

TINY!
SPECTER No. 004
KODAMA
A supernatural tree. It brought all love confessed under its branches to fruition, but the increase of mismatched couples caused chaos in the school. Currently, it's about the size of a broccoli.

キーン
DIIING
コーン
DOOONG
カーン
DAAANG
コーン
DOOONG
SO, HEY, DID YOU HEAR?
THEY SAY THE ENTRANCE TO THE MIDDLE SCHOOL...
...IS HAUNTED.
EARRING: TRAFFIC-SAFETY CHARM
WHEN YOU'RE CHANGING YOUR SHOES, THE GHOST WILL GRAB YOUR ARM.
AND THEN, IT'LL SAY...
HEY.
WHOA!
CUT IT OUT, SATOU!
HUH?
I DIDN'T DO ANY-THING.
BASH
ばし
HUH? THEN —?

DID YOU FORGET ABOUT ME?

MITSUBA (PART 1)

CLAMP

GRIN

YOU'RE HAUNTIN' THE WRONG GUY!

GRAAAAAH!!

FWAM

!?

WHAM
JOLT

SO THE RUMORS ABOUT YOU WERE TRUE, YOU DAMN EVIL SPIRIT.

I'M GONNA CAPTURE YOU, AND... UM?

...A UNIFORM?
HE WAS A STUDENT HERE?

交通
封

SIGN: GIRLS' RESTROOM

...HEY, KID.

WHATCHA GOT THERE?

HE'S AN EVIL SPIRIT WHO WAS CAUSING TROUBLE AT THE MIDDLE SCHOOL ENTRANCE, AND I CAUGHT HIM!!

HMM...

MMPH!

MMPH!

AND NOW YOU'RE GOING TO EXORCISE HIM?

!?

JOLT

ビク

UH...
I STOPPED DOING THAT KINDA THING.

SO!
I WAS WONDERING... THERE'S GOTTA BE SOME OTHER WAY WE CAN DEAL WITH THE PROBLEM, RIGHT!?
SOME OTHER WAY? HMM...

STAAARE
じぃぃ

......

WELL.
HE'S PROBABLY HERE BECAUSE OF SOME UNFINISHED BUSINESS, RIGHT?
SO MAYBE YOU JUST NEED TO FINISH THAT FOR HIM?
OF COURSE!
BADUM ドキ
BADUM ドキ
BADUM ドキ

YANK
NOW THAT WE KNOW THAT, THIS SHOULD BE EASY!

LET'S GO, EVIL SPIRIT!
WE'RE GONNA TAKE CARE OF YOUR UNFINISHED BUSINESS!!
DASH

WILL HE BE OKAY WITHOUT US?
HE'LL BE FINE.

YOU'D PROBABLY BETTER STAY AWAY FROM THAT GHOST.
HE'S NOT ALL THAT DANGEROUS RIGHT NOW, THOUGH...
AND EVEN IF SOME-THING DOES HAPPEN...
WELL, THEN...

...ALL THAT MEANS...

...IS I'LL HAVE A LITTLE MORE WORK TO DO.

THIS GUY LOOKS PRETTY WEAK...
...SO I GUESS I'LL TAKE THE BIG, TOUGH GUY APPROACH...
RIP

OKAY! TELL ME ALL ABOUT THIS UNFINISHED BUSINESS OF YOURS!
OWWW!

I'LL SOLVE IT IN A FLASH!

AND THEN, YOU CAN HAPPILY GET THE HELL OUTTA HERE AND GO TO THE NEXT LIFE!

SPARKLE

SPARKLE

SPARKLE

TA-DAA

SHUT IT, MR. HELLA-LAME TRAFFIC-SAFETY EARRING.

SCOFF

交通

THAT STUPID EARRING!!
ROAR

"TRAFFIC SAFETY"!? AS IF!
YOUR BRAIN'S ALREADY BEEN IN AN ACCI-DENT!!
交通
SPIN AROUND A HUNDRED TIMES AND DROP DEAD!!

SFX: STAGGER

TAKING ADVANTAGE OF MY DELICATE FRAME TO HAVE YOUR WAY WITH ME...

PERVERT! PREDATOR!!

!?

STUPID DUMMY-HEAD!!

CRY

I KNOW WHAT YOU'RE UP TO!!

YOU'RE GONNA ROUGH ME UP, ALL BECAUSE I'M SUCH AN ADORABLE LITTLE GHOST!

CRY

I-I'M NOT...

LIKE IN THOSE DIRTY VIDEOS!

HUH?

CRY

LIKE IN THOSE DIRTY VIDEOS!

NO, I...

TWENTY MINUTES LATER

GET IT OUT OF YOUR SYSTEM YET...?
RANT FATIGUE
HFF...!
HFF...!
...YOU.
I-I'M, UH...
AH!
NO! I CAN'T SHOW WEAKNESS TO AN EVIL SPIRIT!!
I HAVE TO SHOW HIM THE DIGNITY OF THE MINAMOTO LINE...!!

MY NAME IS KOU MINAMOTO!

THE SECOND SON IN AN ANCIENT AND HONORABLE EXORCIST FAMILY!

EXORCIST FAMILY...?

WHOA...YOU WATCH WAY TOO MUCH ANIME.

IRK

I REALLY WANNA EXORCISE THIS GUY ...!!

STAY AWAY...

SCARY ...

SO?
WHAT DOES THE SELF-PROCLAIMED EXORCIST (LOL) WITH A DWEEBY TRAFFIC-SAFETY EARRING WANT WITH ME?
IT'S "KOU"!
...THE LAME-O PERVERT WITH A TRAFFIC-SAFETY EARRING.
"KOU"!!!
DAMMIT, I'M SERIOUSLY GONNA ERASE YOU!
PLEASE DON'T BE VIOLENT.
WHIMPER

YOU HAVE FIVE SECONDS TO TELL ME YOUR NAME AND UNFINISHED BUSINESS.
OR I'LL ERASE YOU RIGHT HERE AND NOW.
SCREAM
I'M SORRY, I'M SORRY!!
SO YOUR NAME IS...?
......
...MITSUBA.
HOW OLD ARE YOU?
SILENCE
YEAR IN SCHOOL?
SULK
WHAT'S YOUR UNFINISHED BUSINESS?

......

AAAH, STOP IT! A PICTURE!

IT'S A PHOTOGRAPH!!

빈 ZAP

A PICTURE?

I...
I THINK......
COUGH

YOU CAN'T JUST ASK ME ABOUT MY UNFINISHED BUSINESS. I HONESTLY DON'T HAVE AN ANSWER OFF THE TOP OF MY HEAD...
BUT BEFORE I DIED, THERE WAS A PICTURE I WANTED TO TAKE...I THINK.
UH-HUH...
...IF YOU'RE REALLY GOING TO HELP ME FINISH MY BUSINESS...
...THEN MY CAMERA WAS DONATED TO THE PHOTOGRAPHY CLUB.
GO TO THE CLUBROOM AND GET IT.

カシャ
SNAP
Nikomi
FM10

MITSUBA.
ピヨ
CHEEP
ピヨ
CHEEP
カシャ
SNAP
HEY, MITSUBA.
HMMM?
カシャ
SNAP

THIS HURTS!
YOU LOOK GOOD UNDER MY FEET. LOLOLOLOL!
DAMMIT, YOU'RE GONNA REGRET THIS, I SWEAR!!
BIRD SEED

I MEAN...
...THIS BETTER REALLY BE THE PICTURE YOU WANTED TO TAKE!

UH-HUH, THIS IS TOTALLY IT.

THAT'S THE FOURTH TIME YOU'VE SAID THAT.

PHOTO SHOOT DIGEST

1 KITTENS

PFFT! HA!

MEW!

MEW!

← MOTHER

WAAAH!

CATNIP

2 BEEHIVE

WHOOHOO!

BUZZ

BUZZ

BUZZ

BUZZ

WAAAAH!

3 RAINBOW

HA HA HA HA!

WHOO!

WAAAAH!

CAN'T WE JUST WRAP THIS UP?

WHAAAT? BUT I THOUGHT YOU WERE GONNA STICK WITH ME UNTIL I FOUND THE PICTURE I WANTED TO TAKE.

STRETCH

OR WHAT? IS THE EXORCIST FROM AN ANCIENT AND DIGNIFIED LINE WITH THE DORKY-ASS TRAFFIC-SAFETY EARRING...

...REALLY A PROMISE-BREAKING LIAR WITH AN UNCOOL TRAFFIC-SAFETY...

PFFT!

AAAAAAAH!!

DON'T BE SO FULL OF YOURSELF...

AAAAH! I'M DISAPPEARING! I'M GONNA DISAPPEEEEEEEEAR!!

ZZZZZAP

SO, HEY...

...YOU'VE ONLY TAKEN PICTURES OF ANIMALS AND SCENERY.

WHAT ABOUT PEOPLE?

YOU DON'T WANT TO TAKE PICTURES OF CLUBS AT PRACTICE OR ANYTHING?

WHOO-HOO!

YEAH!

HUH?

...

ALL RIGHT!

HIT IT!!

BEAM
ぱっ
WHAT ABOUT ME!?
I'LL BE THE BEST SUBJECT EVER!
......

I'LL PASS.
WHY!!?
NO THANK YOU.
ガーン!!
CLAAANG
I'M PRETTY PARTICULAR ABOUT THE PICTURES I TAKE...
IT'S MY POLICY TO ONLY TAKE PICTURES OF THINGS I LIKE... OR THINGS I THINK ARE IMPORTANT TO ME...
SORRY.
UTTER REJECTION!!
THAT HURTS!!

TEP
TEP
TEP
OH?

KOU, IT'S YOU!
WHAT'RE YOU DOING OUT HERE?
YOKOO...
UH... A PHOTO SHOOT, I GUESS?
PHOTOS ...?
NEVER A DULL MOMENT WITH YOU, HUH?

HMM?
THAT CAMERA...
Nikomi
MITSUBA
ISN'T THAT MITSUBA-KUN'S?
交通
......
...YOU KNOW HIM?
WE WERE IN THE SAME CLASS IN OUR FIRST YEAR...
BUT...

IT MUST HAVE BEEN SOMETIME THIS LAST WINTER...
HE DIED IN AN ACCIDENT OR SOMETHING.
WHAT...?
I WAS NEVER REALLY THAT CLOSE TO HIM.
BUT YOU WERE IN THAT CLASS TOO, WEREN'T YOU, KOU?
WHAT!?
I-I WAS!?
TURN

......

SURE WERE!

WELL, I GUESS IT'S HARD TO REMEMBER NOW, SINCE WE'RE IN DIFFERENT CLASSES...

...HEY, WHAT'RE YOU LOOKING AT?

MITSUBA... THAT MITSUBA ...?

NICE TO MEET YOU.

BADGE: NEW STUDENT

I'M MITSUBA.

WE'LL BE SITTING IN ALPHABETICAL ORDER FOR A WHILE, SO I GUESS I'M IN FRONT OF YOU.

LET'S BE FRIENDS, OKAY?

ご入学

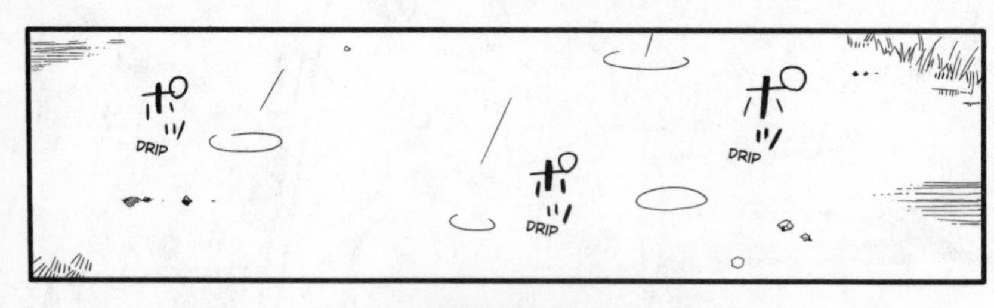
ポツ
DRIP
ポツ
DRIP
ポツ
DRIP

バサ
FLAP
ポツ
DRIP

MITSU ...
I TRIED TALKING TO...
...EVERY PERSON I EVER THOUGHT WAS MY FRIEND.

BUT NONE OF THEM KNEW IT WAS ME.
...ONLY I...
...REMEMBERED.

MITSUBA (PART 2)

I TRIED TALKING TO...

...EVERY PERSON I EVER THOUGHT WAS MY FRIEND.

BUT NONE OF THEM KNEW IT WAS ME.

......

...IT'S STARTING TO RAIN.
LET'S GO INSIDE.

I...
...WAS BULLIED WHEN I WAS IN ELEMENTARY SCHOOL.

FOR "LOOKING LIKE A GIRL," BEING "SASSY"...
STUPID REASONS LIKE THAT.
OH YEAH...
Nikomi

WOULD YOU NOT AGREE, PLEASE?
S- SORRY.

ANYWAY...
THAT'S WHY I WANTED TO TRY TO MAKE THINGS WORK OUT IN MIDDLE SCHOOL.
I'D TAKE THE HINT—I'D BE NICE SO NO ONE WOULD CALL ME SASSY.
I'D BE FRIENDLY—BUT NOT PUSHY—WITH EVERYONE.

AND THIS IS WHERE IT GOT ME.
"A BORING GUY WHO BARELY STANDS OUT FROM THE BACKGROUND."

NOBODY BULLIED ME...
...BUT I COULDN'T MAKE ANY FRIENDS EITHER.

DID YOU FORGET ABOUT ME?
...THAT EXPLAINS IT.
......

HE'S SASSY.
HUH?
LOOKS LIKE A GIRL.
SARCASTIC.
つら
RAMBLE
JUST A—
SELFISH.
つら
RAMBLE
HUH?
UM?
OBSESSED WITH HIS CAMERA.
HAS AN ANNOYING VOICE.
GOES EMO SOMETIMES.
つら
RAMBLE
WHA...?
AND IS ONLY FAKE-NICE.
WHAT'S YOUR DEAL!?
IF ANYBODY ASKS ME, "WHAT KIND OF A GUY IS SOUSUKE MITSUBA?"...
...THAT'S WHAT I'M GONNA TELL 'EM.

WHA...?
I'M SORRY...
...FOR NOT REALIZING IT WAS YOU.

I JUST DIDN'T RECOGNIZE YOU BECAUSE YOU WERE SO DIFFERENT FROM WHEN WE MET IN FIRST YEAR.

AND...
...YOU KNOW...

...I DON'T THINK YOU HAD TO FORCE ANYTHING.
JUST BE YOURSELF...
TAP

I DO THINK YOU'VE GOT A WARPED PERSONALITY.

BUT I DON'T HATE IT.

...A LOT OF GOOD THAT DOES ME NOW.
...YEAH.

MINA-MOTO-KUN.
HMM?
IF I WERE STILL ALIVE...
...DO YOU THINK WE COULD HAVE BEEN FRIENDS?

2
TURN

CAN'T WE STILL BE FRIENDS, EVEN IF YOU ARE DEAD?
交通
Nikomi

SNAP
カシャ
OH?
WHAT'D YOU TAKE A PICTURE OF?

THE SKY?
...WHO KNOWS?
Nikomi
SOMETHING IMPORTANT TO ME... MAYBE?

HMM...?
IT DOESN'T MATTER! LET'S GO.
HUH?
PUSH PUSH
YOU CAN HELP ME DEVELOP THEM TOMORROW!

AND THEN...
...I THINK I'LL BE OKAY.
!
...YOU THINK SO?

SIGN: EMERGENCY EXIT

WELL, OKAY! LET'S PICK THIS UP TOMORROW!
CREAK
YEAH.
I'LL BE WAITING AT THE ENTRAN—
SHUT
MIII-TSUUU-BA-KUN.

IT BOTHERS ME WHEN YOU DO THESE THINGS.

HANAKO ...?
GRIN
ニコッ
......NO, IT'S NOT HIM.
WHO IS THIS KID...!?
STRIDE
スッ
PAT
TRYING TO MOVE ON... WITHOUT A WORD TO ME...?

WE CAN'T HAVE THAT.
ずる…
SHLUP
HUH?
MITSUBA

SHUNK
ズブ

SLURP
ぐにゃ
WH—
FWUMP
べしゃ
WH—

LEAP

WHAT THE HELL ARE YOU DOING!!?

SWISH

WHAM

REMEMBER, MITSUBA?
YOU ASKED ME TO GRANT YOUR WISH!
URG...
SLIDE

YOU SAID, "I WANT TO STAY IN EVERYONE'S MEMORIES."
......
GRAB

NOW YOU HAVE JUST ONE PERSON, AND YOU'RE HAPPY WITH THAT?

NO, YOU'RE NOT.

WHO DO YOU THINK YOU ARE...?
DON'T YOU DARE TOUCH MITSUBA ...

DON'T YOU LAY A HAND ON MY FRIEND ...!!

......
...WOW.

!!
WHOOSH

KAPOW

AH...
WOOZY

I AM A SUPER-NATURAL.
FOR THE RIGHT PRICE, I WILL GRANT THE WISH OF WHOEVER SUMMONS ME.
AMANE GRANTS THE WISHES OF THE LIVING...
...AND I GRANT THE WISHES OF THE DEAD.
HE MADE A WISH, AND I ANSWERED.
AND NOW, I'M GOING TO MAKE HIS WISH COME TRUE.

CLUNK

AND I'M GOING TO DO IT MY WAY.

A RADIO ...?
WHAT'S HE GOING TO...?
WAVER
OKAY, MITSUBA.
IT'S TIME TO GRANT YOUR WISH!

SAKURA!
WE'RE ALL READY!
Got it.
CRACKLE
KZH
KZH
KZH

BADUM
...Have you heard this rumor?
"The Bent-Neck Boy at the School Entrance."
!?
HUH...?
UH...
They say a ghost with a broken neck...
...appears at the entrance to the middle school division.

He is a very lonely ghost.
So he might talk to you too. He'll say...
"Hey...
"...DID YOU FORGET ABOUT ME?"
AH!
WAH!
ZH
...!
ZH
ZH

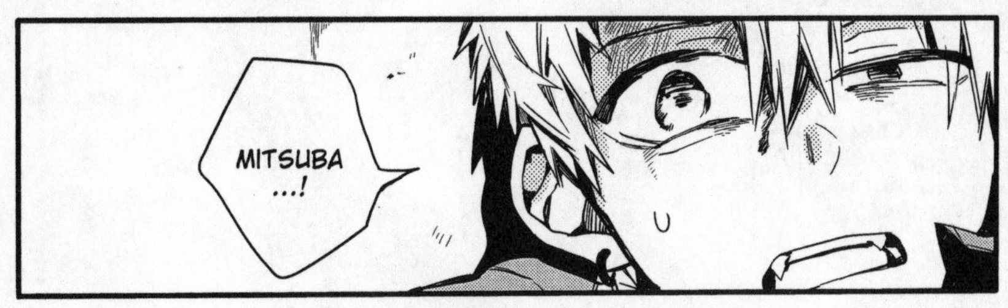

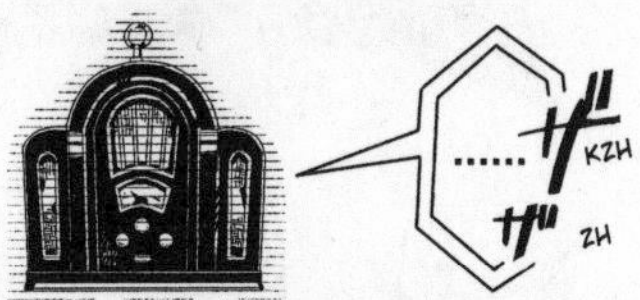

SWIVEL

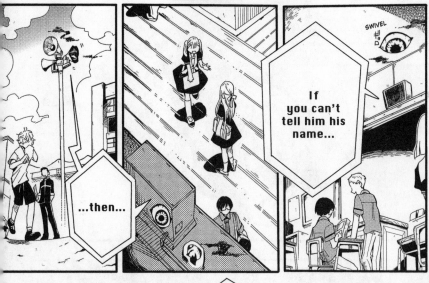

If you can't tell him his name...

...then...

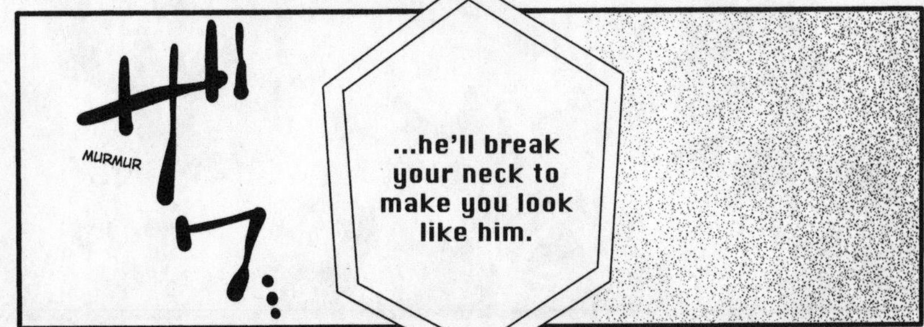

DID YOU HEAR? A FRIEND OF A FRIEND TOLD ME...
PSST
EWW! THAT'S DISGUSTING!
PSST
WAS IT THE MIDDLE SCHOOL ENTRANCE?
YOUR NECK!
HE'LL BREAK YOUR NECK...!
PSST
THAT'S SCAAARY...
NGH.
WAH.
NO!
AH...

THIS CAN'T BE REAL.

MITSUBA...!

ドクン BADUM

ドクン BADUM

MINAMOTO... KUN...

ザザッ CRAK

ザッ CRACKLE

ザ CRACKLE

ザザッ CRACKLE

ザ CRACKLE

...THERE.

カチ CLICK

NOW...

...NO ONE WILL EVER FORGET YOU.

ズズズ THRUM

GOOD FOR YOU...
...MITSUBA!

TOILET

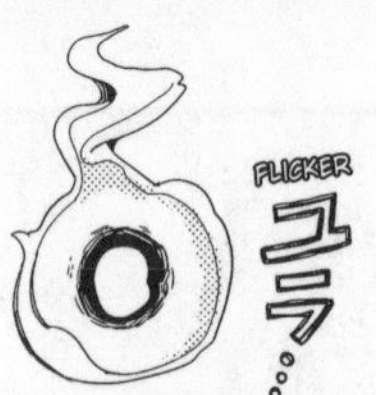
FLICKER
ユラ…

SISSS
ヒュルルル
IS SOMETHING WRONG, HAKU-JOUDAI?

THE SCHOOL'S SEVEN MYSTERIES...
...SAY THEY MAINTAIN CORRECT RELATIONSHIPS BETWEEN HUMANS AND SUPER-NATURALS.

BUT WHO NEEDS THAT?
HUMANS AND SUPER-NATURALS SHOULD JUST BE HOWEVER THEY WANT.
IF THAT'S ENOUGH TO BREAK THE WORLD...
...THEN IT'S BETTER OFF BROKEN.

DON'T YOU THINK?

SPOOK 20
MITSUBA (PART 3)

ず ZH
ず ZH
MITSUBA ...?
ず ZH

MITSUBA'S WISH WAS A LITTLE VAGUE!

"I DON'T KNOW WHAT I WANT TO DO ON THE NEAR SHORE.
"BUT I DON'T WANT IT TO END LIKE THIS.
"I WANT TO STAY IN EVERYONE'S MEMORIES."

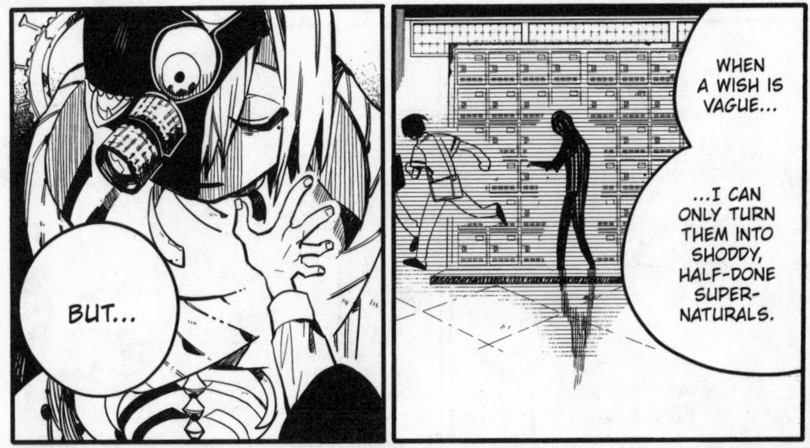
WHEN A WISH IS VAGUE...
...I CAN ONLY TURN THEM INTO SHODDY, HALF-DONE SUPER-NATURALS.
BUT...

...NOW I CAN DO BETTER.
AND I HAVE YOU TO THANK FOR IT.

ME...?

YUP.

YOU DREW OUT MITSUBA'S REAL WISH FOR ME.

THE STRONGER THE WISH... THE REGRET, THE MORE DISTINCT AND POWERFUL A SUPERNATURAL CAN BECOME.

THIS WAS MITSUBA'S WISH—

"I WANT FRIENDS.

"I WANT TO STAY WITH MY FRIENDS...

"...FOREVER AND EVER."
WH-WHAT THE HELL ARE YOU TALKING ABOUT!?
CRACKLE
QUIT YOUR YAKKING...
...AND TURN MITSUBA BACK, DAMMIT!!
BESIDES, I THOUGHT MITSUBA'S UNFINISHED BUSINESS WAS TO TAKE PICTURES...
HMPH.

BUT, Y'KNOW ...
WAS IT REALLY, MITSUBA?
...THE MORE PEOPLE YOU GET TO REMEMBER YOU...
...THE LONGER YOU GET TO STAY HERE.
OH, I HAVE AN IDEA!
IF YOU MAKE HIM JUST LIKE YOU...
...YOU COULD BE TOGETHER FOREVER, HUH?
WHA...?
ピク
TWITCH

DON'T WORRY.
IT DOESN'T MATTER IF WHAT YOU WANT IS GOOD OR BAD OR WHO YOU HURT TO GET IT.
I WILL FORGIVE EVERY-THING.
TOUCH
THE PRICE OF THIS WISH IS YOUR MIND.
NOW NOTHING STANDS IN YOUR WAY.
SO GO!
FIGHT THE LAWS OF THIS WORLD.
LET ME SEE YOU STRUGGLE ...
... MITSUBA.
SWAY
MI-TSU-BA ...!

SHRRR
!

ACK!?
ギュルルルル
WHIIIIRRR
UH!
みしっ
CREAK
ギチギチ
TIGHTEN
TIGHTEN
MITSU-
BA...
STOP
IT!
......
SNAP
OUT OF
IT...!
めきっ
SNAP
EYAAAAARGH!
MITSUBA
!!

STOP IT!
CAN'T YOU HEAR ME ...!?
CREAK
CREAK
ぎら
CINCH

AND I HAVE YOU TO THANK FOR IT.

......

W-WAS ...

WAS I... WRONG...?

HEY...

COME ON...SAY SOMETHING...

WHAM

OW!

ドサッ

THUD

スト

TMP

IT'S AMANE!

ぱぁっ

BEAM

HOW MANY YEARS HAS IT BEEN?

TEN? TWENTY...?

OH!

THAT'S RIGHT—WE MET ON THE ROOF JUST THE OTHER DAY!

AH HA HA!

WHY ARE YOU DOING THIS...?

TSUKASA !!

BECAUSE I LIKE IT.
THE LOOK ON PEOPLE'S FACES WHEN THEY DECIDE TO STOP HOLDING BACK.

YOURS WAS REALLY GOOD TOO, AMANE.

BACK WHEN YOU KILLED ME.

......!
...YEAH, THAT'S A GOOD FACE.

I LOVE YOU, AMANE.

LET'S PLAY TOGETHER...
...LIKE WE USED TO.

OKAY?
SMIRK

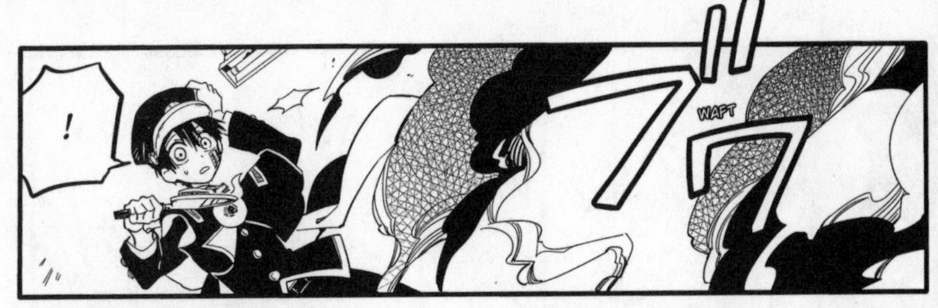
ブワ
WAFT
!

ニュルル
SHRRR

......

MITSU-
BA!
HEY!
MITSU-
BA!!

KID.
HANAKO...

HEY, YOU...
...CAN FIX HIM, RIGHT...?

LIKE THE MISAKI STAIRS AND STUFF.

YOU CAN PUT HIM BACK...

......

CLENCH

MITSU-BA!
YOU... YOU...
THIS ISN'T YOU!
THE MITSUBA I KNOW...
SOUSUKE MITSUBA WAS...

...S—
SASSY.
LOOKED LIKE A GIRL.
SARCASTIC.
SELFISH.

AND...
AND HIS VOICE WAS ANNOYING.
SOMETIMES, HE WAS EMO, AND HE WAS ONLY FAKE-NICE.
HE WAS OBSESSED WITH CAMERAS.
AND...!

AND HE WAS MY FRIEND ...!!

NO...

KID.

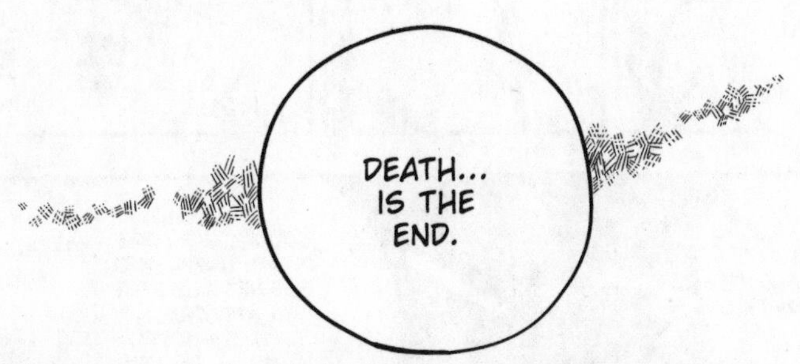
DEATH... IS THE END.

YOU CAN BECOME A SPIRIT AND WANDER THE LAND OF LIVING...
...BUT THAT'S NOT A CONTINUATION OF LIFE.

ONCE YOU'VE DIED, IT'S OVER.
THERE'S NOTHING AFTER THAT.
YOU CAN'T GO ANYWHERE FROM THERE.

IT DOESN'T MATTER HOW DEEP YOUR REGRETS ARE OR HOW MUCH YOU WISH THINGS WERE DIFFERENT.
IF YOU COULDN'T DO SOMETHING IN LIFE...

...YOU CAN'T DO IT AFTER YOU'RE DEAD.

THAT'S HOW THIS WORLD IS MADE, AND IF YOU TRY TO FIGHT IT...
...THIS IS HOW YOU END UP.

...I THOUGHT...
...IF ANYONE COULD TAKE CARE OF HIS UNFINISHED BUSINESS...SEVER HIS ATTACHMENT TO THIS SHORE... IT WOULD BE YOU.
BUT IT LOOKS LIKE IT BACKFIRED.

IT'S NO USE.
YOU CAN'T BE SO KIND TO THE DEAD.
...

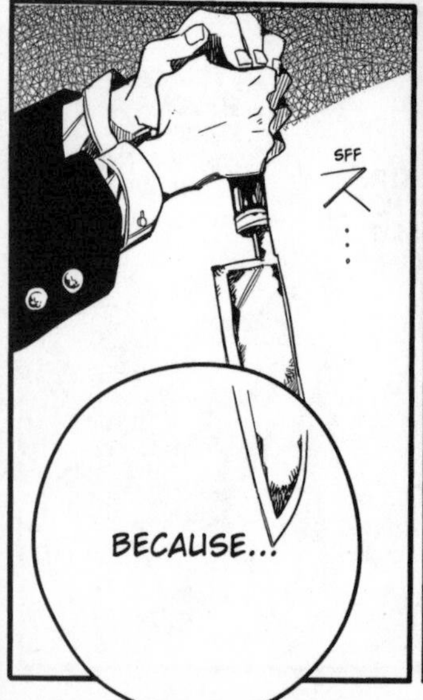
SFF
ス...
BECAUSE...

...WE
HAVE NO
FUTURE
ANYMORE.

Nikomi
コト…
CLUNK

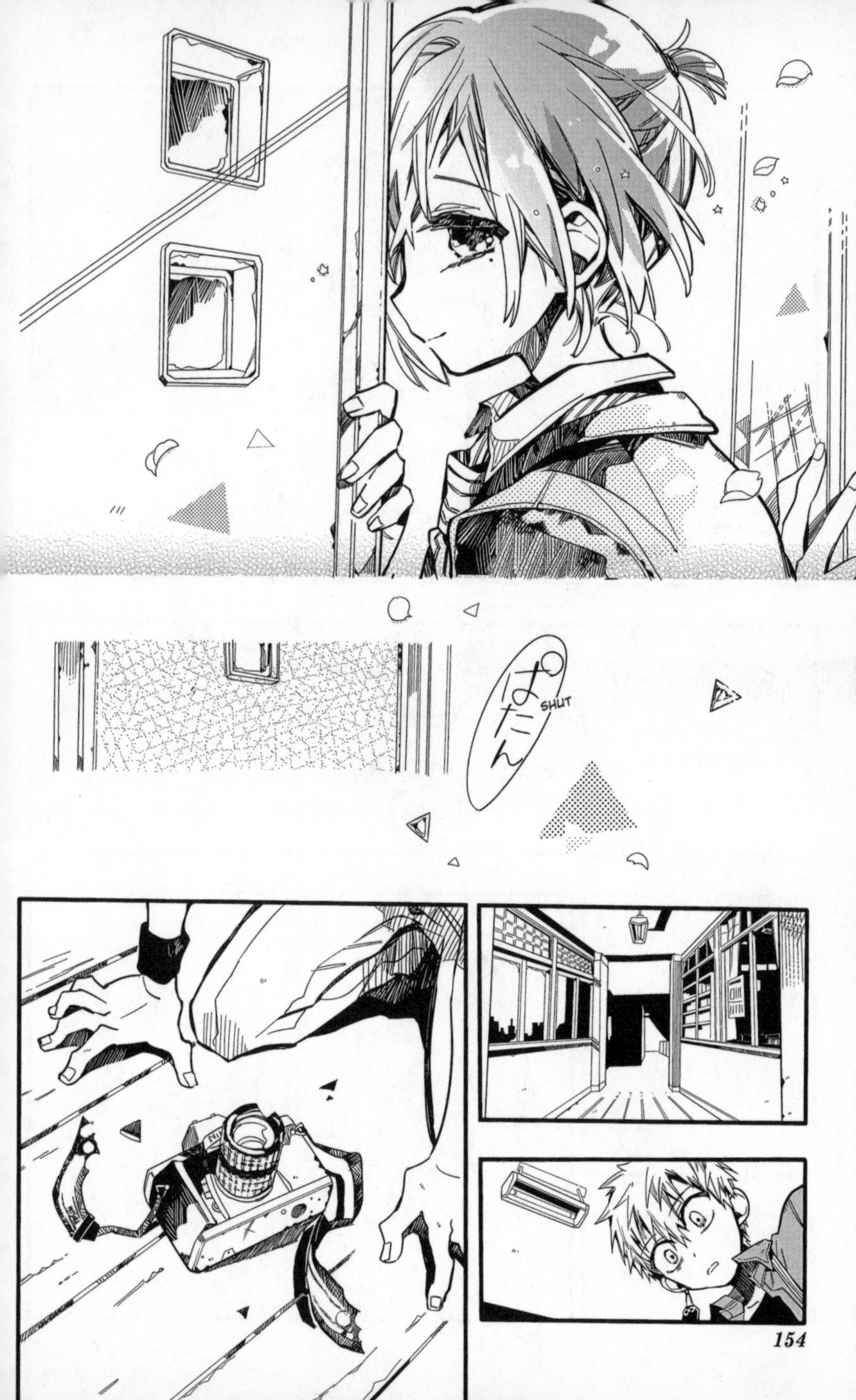
ぱたん
SHUT

くる TURN
....
...MORE.
?
THERE...
THERE SHOULD'VE BEEN SOMETHING MORE.
IF I WERE STRONGER, LIKE TERU-NII...
SOMETHING I COULD DO... SOMETHING I COULD'VE DONE FOR HIM...
...IT WOULDN'T HAVE TURNED OUT THIS WAY!

DON'T LET IT TROUBLE YOU, KID.
I'M PRETTY SURE DESTRUCTION IS THE ONLY SALVATION FOR THE DEAD.
IT'S BETTER THIS WAY.
GRAB
NO, IT'S NOT!
BESIDES—
IT'S NOT BETTER!!
DISAP-PEARING IS THE ONLY WAY TO BE SAVED!?
CUT THE CRAP!!!

THE GUY WHO DID THAT TO MITSUBA...
I SWEAR I'LL MAKE HIM PAY...!!
......

...I SEE.

MINAMOTO
源

ROAD: STOP

HANAKO WAS RIGHT, SORT OF.

THERE ARE RULES TO HOW THE WORLD'S SET UP.
YOUR AVERAGE PERSON PROBABLY CAN'T DO ANYTHING ABOUT THEM.
I GET THAT MUCH.

BUT I CAN SEE SUPER-NATURALS— I CAN SEE THINGS THAT AREN'T PART OF THIS WORLD.

I WAS GIVEN THE POWER TO DO SOMETHING ABOUT THOSE THINGS.

THAT MUST MEAN I CAN DO SOMETHING ABOUT THESE THINGS WE SUPPOSEDLY CAN'T DO ANYTHING ABOUT.

I STILL THINK THAT, EVEN NOW.

...I DON'T GET IT.

STARE

じー

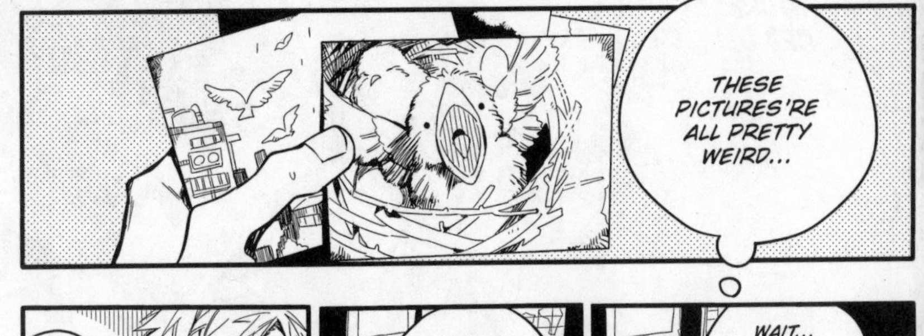
THESE PICTURES'RE ALL PRETTY WEIRD...

WAIT... MAYBE PICTURES LIKE THIS ARE GOOD ...?
BEATS ME...
ゴロ
ROLL
...
I DO KINDA GET THE FEELING THEY'RE ARTISTIC...
YEAH.
GRADE IN ART. F
HUH?

WHAT'D YOU TAKE A PICTURE OF?

......WHO KNOWS?

SOMETHING IMPORTANT TO ME...

...MAYBE?

FWUMP
ばふ

MITSUBA...

ザザーン
SPLASH
SPLASH

ブク
GLUB

チリーン
CHIIING

ブク
GLUB
ブク
GLUB

CHIIING
チリーン
CHIIING
チリーン

チリーン
CHIIING

I SEE.
MM-HMM.
MM-HMM.
MM-HMM.
MM-HMM.

...WELL, WELL. HOW DREADFUL.
IS THAT WHAT'S HAPPENING ON THE NEAR SHORE?

A SUPERNATURAL BEING DISRUPTING THE SUPERNATURAL RUMORS...

MM-HMM.

SHE MAY BE AN IMBECILE, BUT THAT GIRL IS TECHNICALLY ONE OF US.
I WANTED TO GIVE HER SHELTER HERE BEFORE ANYTHING HAPPENED.

BUT IT WOULD SEEM I AM FORCED TO GIVE UP ON THAT HOPE...

ブク
GLUB
ブク
GLUB

キーン
DIIING
コーン
DOOONG
カーン
DAAANG
コーン
DOOONG
KAMOME ACADEMY
かもめ学園

TREMBLE
ぶる

TREMBLE
ぶる

Idol-Raising Game
NNGH... YOUR FINAL CONCERT WAS A SUCCESS. CONGRATS!
I'M HAPPY FOR YOU... TRULY... HAPPY FOR YOU...
THE CONCERT WAS A HUGE SUCCESS!
THANK YOU, PRODUCER YASHIRO!!

NENE-CHAN!
PAT
ぽん
AIEEEE!

WH-WH-WH-WH-WH-WH-WHAT?
TEE-HEE-HEE! GUESS WHAT!

YOU'VE BEEN SUMMONED!
BY A HOT UPPER-CLASSMAN!
WHAT!?

SEE? OVER THERE!
SQUEE
きゃあ
HMM, I'LL TELL YOU IF YOU GIVE ME YOUR NUMBER.
WHAT YEAR ARE YOU IN, SENPAI?
EEEE!
OH OOOO!
SQUEE

OH, NENE-CHAN! YOU'RE SO POPULAR...!

C-COME ON...! I AM NOOOT...!

BUT MAYBE IT COULD POSSIBLY LEAD TO...?
わく
EXCITED
1
HOT GUY
I LOVE YOU.
2
HOT GUY
GO OUT WITH ME.
3
KING
MARRY ME.
EXCITED
わく
EXCITED
わく

COMING THROUGH!

OH.

YO.

TO BE CONTINUED IN TOILET-BOUND HANAKO-KUN 5!

TEN-TIMES GAME, PART 2

KID, SAY "HELLO" TEN TIMES FAST.

YOU GOT IT!!!

HELLO, HELLO, HELLO!

HELLO, HELLO!

HELLO, HELLO, HELLO, HELLO, HELLO !!!!

I DID IT!!!

AND THIS IS!?

ELLO !!!

DUDUN ドッ

AH HA HA!

KOU...

TEN-TIMES SERVICE

TRY SAYING "PRINCE" TEN TIMES FAST!

WHAT?

WELL, WHATEVER.

PRINCE, PRINCE, PRINCE, PRINCE, PRINCE, PRINCE, PRINCE.

PRINCE.

PRINCE.

PRINCE.

THERE.

YOU GOT TO HEAR AN ADORABLE BOY LIKE ME CALL YOU "PRINCE" TEN TIMES...

ARE YOU HAPPY NOW?

YOU...

...PERVERT!!

HUH ...?

TEN-TIMES CANCEL

TRANSLATION NOTES

Common Honorifics

no honorific: Indicates familiarity or closeness; if used without permission or reason, addressing someone in this manner would constitute an insult.

-san: The Japanese equivalent of Mr./Mrs./Miss. If a situation calls for politeness, this is the fail-safe honorific.

-sama: Conveys great respect; may also indicate that the social status of the speaker is lower than that of the addressee.

-kun: Used most often when referring to boys, this indicates affection or familiarity. Occasionally used by older men among their peers, but it may also be used by anyone referring to a person of lower standing.

-chan: An affectionate honorific indicating familiarity used mostly in reference to girls; also used in reference to cute persons or animals of either gender.

-senpai: A suffix used to address upperclassmen or more experienced coworkers.

-sensei: A respectful term for teachers, artists, or high-level professionals.

Page 14

In Japan, the story of "The Little Mermaid" is known as *Ningyo-hime,* or "The Mermaid Princess," which is likely the inspiration for Nene's royal treatment.

Page 29

The turtle with a seat on its back is a reference to the Japanese folktale of Tarou Urashima, who was taken to the undersea Palace of the Dragon God on the back of a giant turtle as thanks for saving the daughter of the Emperor of the Sea.

Page 31

Fish prints (*Gyotaku*) are a traditional form of Japanese art practiced by fishermen to record their catches. They paint one side of the fish with ink and then rub it onto paper to create a life-size print.

Page 164

The picture of the mustachioed puffer fish is an *iei,* a memorial portrait displayed at funerals. *Iei* are always somewhat-recent headshots on neutral backgrounds and frequently have black ribbons draped over them like in this panel. Since open-casket funerals are rare in Japan, the function of the *iei* is to remind the family and other mourners of what the deceased was like in life and to reassure them the deceased is now happy and at peace, which is why the expression used for the *iei* is usually fairly cheerful.

Page 169

The original version of this tongue twister relies on the similarity of the Japanese words for "knee" (*hiza*) and "elbow" (*hiji*). By making the other person say "pizza" ten times fast and then asking what the word for "elbow" is, the other person says the similar sounding body part that rhymes with "pizza" on autopilot instead. In the second sketch, Kou is now aware of this trick and focuses on saying the second syllable right, but forgets about changing the first and blurts out *piji,* which is just a nonsense word. The other two are riffing on this idea and do not actually have any tongue twister involved.

Page 175

Bekko candy are traditional Japanese hard candies, an old-school pick in keeping with Tsuchigomori's actual age.

Hanako-kun

What's your favorite snack?

Donuts.

What's your biggest concern lately?

I can't beat the Mokke at cards

Nene Yashiro

What's your favorite snack?

Strawberry-filled rice cakes.

What's your biggest concern lately?

I have terrible luck with men.

Kou Minamoto

Q What's your favorite snack?

Sweet-potato jellies.

Q What's your biggest concern lately?

I ain't got no concerns!!!

Mitsuba

Q What's your favorite snack?

Flan.

Q What's your biggest concern lately?

I can't build any muscle.

Teru Minamoto

What's your favorite snack?

Sweet potatoes.

What's your biggest concern lately?

I'm sad when I think of my brother not needing me anyr

Mokke

What's your favorite snack?

Candy.

What's your biggest concern lately?

They won't let us be part of the Seven Mysteries.

Yako

Q What's your favorite snack?

Sweet-bean-jelly sandwiches.

Q What's your biggest concern lately?

It's so hard to groom myself.

Tsuchigomori

Q What's your favorite snack?

Bekko candy.

Q What's your biggest concern lately?

It's pretty hard living a double life as a teacher and supernatural.

TEACH ME, MITSUBA-KUN
— LOVE STORIES —

☆ SPECIAL THANKS ☆

NATSUMI-CHAN

EKE-CHAN

OMAYU-TAN

YUUKI

RINGO-CHAN

RUI-CHAN

REYU-CHAN

MY EDITOR, IMANITY

COVER DESIGN, SUZUKI-SAMA

☆ AND YOU ☆

Toilet-bound Hanako-Kun 4

AidaIro

Translation: Alethea Nibley and Athena Nibley
Lettering: Jesse Moriarty

Yen Press
150 West 30th Street, 19th Floor
New York, NY 10001

Visit us at yenpress.com • facebook.com/yenpress • twitter.com/yenpress • yenpress.tumblr.com • instagram.com/yenpress

First Yen Press Print Edition: July 2020
Originally published as an ebook in February 2018 by Yen Press.

Yen Press is an imprint of Yen Press, LLC.
The Yen Press name and logo are trademarks of Yen Press, LLC.

The publisher is not responsible for websites (or their content) that are not owned by the publisher.

Library of Congress Control Number: 2019953610

ISBN: 978-1-9753-1136-0 (paperback)

10 9 8 7 6 5 4 3 2 1

BVG

Printed in the United States of America